catherine stone 8 may 5 –
1994

For Violet Collings
with love ✗ ✗

Though polar bears live around the North pole
and penguins live around the South, in *Pinkie
Leaves Home*, anything is possible.

Copyright © 1991 by Peter O'Donnell

Library of Congress Cataloging-in-Publication Data
O'Donnell, Peter.
Pinkie leaves home / Peter O'Donnell.
p. cm.
Summary: Pinkie the penguin leaves his cold frozen home
for a place in the sun but soon misses his friends.
ISBN 0-590-45485-4
[1. Penguins — Fiction. 2. Friendship — Fiction.] I.Title.
PZ7.0243P1 1992

[E] — dc20   91-19016
                                                              CIP
                                                               AC

12 11 10 9 8 7 6 5 4 3 2 1   2 3 4 5 6/9
Printed in Hong Kong.
First Scholastic printing, May 1992

Pinkie leaves home

Peter O'Donnell

Scholastic Inc. · New York

In a faraway land, among icebergs and glaciers, live the animals who like the cold.

But there is one animal who does not like the cold— Pinkie the Penguin. Poor Pinkie once swam through an oilslick and lost all his feathers, so now he gets very cold and shivers and shakes. On the coldest days the other penguins all gather round Pinkie to help keep him warm, but Pinkie still shivers and shakes.

One day as Pinkie walked around on an iceberg, trying to stay warm, the wind swept a piece of paper straight into his beak.

"Oh!" Pinkie couldn't believe his eyes. "No snow! No ice! It looks hot and there are lots of pink animals— pinker than me—playing in the sea!"

Pinkie ran to show the picture to his friends, and everyone decided that Pinkie had to find this perfect place. So he said goodbye and set off.

As Pinkie swam, he passed a fishing fleet.
"I think I'll rest for a while," he decided and,
climbing aboard a boat, hid quickly in the hold.

Just as he settled down, the hold was suddenly
filled with hundreds of fish. Pinkie could hardly
believe his eyes. All those tasty fish for him to
eat! And eat them he did, every last one.

As night fell, the fishing boat came to rest in the harbor and one very fat pink penguin jumped off and hopped on a nearby train that was waiting to take away the fish.

The train pulled out into the night and as the
hours rolled by, so at first did snowy mountains.

Gradually, as the air got warmer, green
fields and forests came into view.

Then big cities loomed up. But way before that,
Pinkie had fallen asleep to the movement of the train.

When Pinkie awoke, the train
had stopped. He jumped out
onto a sandy beach.

A warm breeze blew and blue waves sparkled.
"Just like the picture!" Sure enough, pink creatures
played in the sea.

As the day went by, the sun got hotter and Pinkie grew thirsty. He followed all the other pink creatures who had lined up at a store to buy ice cream. On the store front was a picture of the cold land and, suddenly, Pinkie was homesick. "I miss my cold home and the other penguins," he thought. "I must find a way to get home."

Pinkie's friends missed Pinkie, too. They wondered how he was and wished he would come back. As they stood talking, waves rolled by and there, on one of the biggest, was Pinkie—surfing home.

Pinkie had brought back souvenirs
and from then on Pinkie wasn't cold
anymore—just very, very cool!